THE HAWK
AND THE
NIGHTINGALE

JENNIFER ALLIS PROVOST

CHAPTER ONE

AMALIE - PRAGUE, PRESENT DAY

THE HAWK HAD ALWAYS considered himself something of a badass. At least, that was what Amalie had heard.

He swept into Prague a few years ago, buying up properties in Old Town while his entourage of flunkies followed him like a pack of lovesick puppies. The shopkeepers and restauranteurs whispered amongst themselves, wondering what The Hawk could be up to. Would he open a gallery, or perhaps a bistro? An elegant clothier, perhaps?

None of those things happened. Instead of doing something useful or beautiful with the many properties he'd acquired, The Hawk opened the loudest, most garish nightclub Prague had ever seen—and in a city with a nightlife as rich and vibrant as Prague's, that was saying something. And then he opened another, and another. Soon enough, The Hawk's clubs were everywhere. Then the worst happened, and The Hawk purchased the vacant warehouse next to Amalie's shop. This latest endeavor created such a cacophony at night it was nearly unbearable, the neon signs were dazzling yet tasteless, but the worst part about the club was its name: The Moravian Ballroom.

"How pretentious," Amalie had said when she first heard what the club was called.

"Yes, it's not nearly as elegant as Bohemian Delights," her assistant, Iveta, deadpanned, referencing the name of Amalie's glassware shop.

Amalie sniffed, and looked toward the Moravian Ballroom's enormous sign. The colors and neon lights were so far out of place among Old Town's Gothic architecture it might as well have been an alien spaceship. "Still, what a waste of the property," she said. "This club is nothing but an eyesore, surely."

"You don't want to dance the night away among the sweaty, half-naked bodies?" Iveta teased.

"I don't dance."

Iveta linked her arm with Amalie's. "I remember one time."

Amalie smiled and leaned her head against Iveta's shoulder. Even though Iveta was the taller of the two, and outwardly fiercer, it was Amalie who would burn the world down to keep them safe. She almost had, once. "Yes. That was a good day."

"You even sang."

Amalie nestled closer to her friend. Her voice was so clear and true she'd been named The Nightingale when she was still young, and the name had stuck. That voice had gotten her into a lot of trouble over the years, but she regretted nothing. Regret was as useless an emotion as worry. "Perhaps I'll sing at this new club?"

Iveta laughed. "As if they could hear you over the speakers."

Amalie glanced at the club's sign again. "Anything is possible."

At first, Amalie tried to pay little to no attention to The Hawk or his new nightclubs. Instead of spending time in nightclubs she preferred the calm interior of her shop, where she sold vintage crystal vases and glass sculptures created by local artisans. She'd always gone out of her way to support all manner of artists, and as a result her shop was filled with many colorful and unique baubles that caught the light, even on overcast days. No matter what else happened in the city, her shop was a haven of peace and solitude.

Or at least it was, until The Hawk extended the Moravian Ballroom's interior all the way to the building adjacent to her shop. Amalie did her best to ignore the construction work that went on 'round the clock, blocking the narrow streets with their deliveries and making her business all but inaccessible to customers. Then the new addition's opening night came, and she realized just how much The Hawk had outdone himself with a state-of-the-art sound system. The music was so loud many of her glass sculptures vibrated off the shelves and smashed onto the floor.

"What a mess," Amalie lamented, when she arrived at the shop the next day.

"We should send that brute a bill for damages," Iveta grumbled, as she swept up the shards.

"No, no," Amalie said. "We don't want to attract his notice."

"Why not?" Iveta demanded. "If we don't at least tell him what happened, he will continue playing that boorish thumping idiotic bass music, and we will continue losing products and profits."

"And what will we accomplish by attracting the notice of the mysterious and wealthy man who only comes out at night?" Amalie countered. "Nothing good, that's what. Trust me, Iveta. This is for the best."

Iveta sniffed. "We'll just see about that."

Two days after Amalie lost almost half of her inventory, she arrived at her shop and found a customer waiting for her. He had his back to the door, so all she saw was a tall man with a mane of sandy blond hair, wearing a black cape and black leather gloves and boots. Amalie glanced around the shop until she found Iveta, who was doing her best to shrink behind the cash register.

"Who is this jackass?" Amalie whispered, for certainly only a jackass would wander around Prague in a black cape and boots at the height of summer. Who did he think he was, Dracula?

Iveta swallowed. "He is The Hawk."

Amalie glanced at the man, then she refocused on Iveta. "And why is The Hawk in my shop?"

"I may have gathered up all of the broken glassware, put it in a box, and sent it to him," Iveta replied. "With a bill for damages."

Amalie blew out a breath. She understood that Iveta was only trying to help, and recoup money for the business. Still, the last thing either of them needed was someone like The Hawk frequenting her shop. "Go to the back," Amalie said. "I will handle this."

Iveta grasped Amalie's hand and squeezed it, then she disappeared into the storeroom. Amalie took a breath to steady her nerves, and approached her lone patron.

"Good evening," she said. "I'm the owner of this shop. May I help you?"

"You often help jackasses?" He turned around, and Amalie understood why he was called The Hawk. His nose was long and elegant, his features refined, and eyes were such a pale blue they pierced you like shards of ice. He very much resembled a raptor swooping down onto his prey.

Amalie wondered if she was his intended prey. *We will just see about that.*

"I have very good hearing," Hawk continued.

"What a wonderful gift," she murmured. "Please forgive Iveta for sending you the damaged items. My wares are delicate, and things often break in the course of the day. I understand that nothing was your fault."

"Perhaps not, but her letter indicated that the music coming from my club shook the very foundations of your establishment," he said. "I believe her exact words were, 'the bass is turned up so loud it's like a chorus of baboons screaming about how stupid they are.'"

Amalie sucked in her lips to keep from laughing. "I will speak to Iveta about using less confrontational language."

"Don't be harsh with her," Hawk said, with a dangerously handsome smile. "I have come to offer you my apologies, and make what restitution I can."

Cold sweat bloomed across Amalie's chest. "No restitution is needed," she said quickly. "Your apology is more than sufficient. Thank you, for delivering it in person."

The Hawk took a step toward Amalie. She held her ground, barely. "I must disagree. Please, come to my club tomorrow night as my guest. I would like the chance to prove to you that I am more than a baboon screaming about my stupidity."

"I don't know," Amalie said, shaking her head.

"Please, little nightingale."

"Nightingale?" she repeated. "Why did you call me that?"

"On occasion, at night, I have heard you sing."

"But where did you hear that name?" she pressed.

"It's what the locals call you," Hawk said, as he took a step back. "I'm sorry, I meant no offense. Is it not a name you go by?"

"It is, though I haven't used it in some time." Amalie watched as Hawk's brows knit together; he was genuinely perplexed by her reaction. Normally she didn't mind being referred to by her old moniker, but Hawk's sudden appearance had put her on edge. She wondered if he'd been sent by her ex-lover, Marek.

Don't be ridiculous. Amalie hadn't heard mention of Marek in so long, their relationship may as well have been a lifetime ago. What's more, ever paranoid Iveta had looked into Hawk's background as soon as he purchased his first property. If there had been there merest hint of Hawk associating with Marek, Iveta would have relocated them to Siberia, rather than risk a confrontation with the evil, sadistic man that once shared her bed.

Iveta had found nothing even remotely suspicious about The Hawk, much to her disappointment, but Amalie had been glad. Now, as Hawk stood over her with his broad shoulders and a gaze that set off sparks in her core, she was very, very glad. It had been a long time since a man had made her feel anything, though it would be wiser to ignore these new, intense emotions Hawk brought out in her.

When had Amalie ever claimed to be wise?

"It's fine," she said at last. "You just surprised me."

Hawk grinned, and she decided she liked the spark. In fact, she wanted to fan that tiny flame and see what came of it. "Was it a good surprise?"

"It was," Amalie replied. "Have you any more planned?"

"A few, but only if you accept my invitation."

"Then, I suppose I must accept. Tomorrow night it is."

CHAPTER TWO

HAWK - PRAGUE,
PRESENT DAY

THE NEXT EVENING, HAWK stood next to the entrance of the Moravian Ballroom, eagerly awaiting Amalie's arrival. He'd long been intrigued by the shopkeeper next door, but gleaning information about her had been all but impossible, and for Hawk nothing was impossible. Money and influence were the best ways to acquire what one wanted, and he wielded both like an expert swordsman. And yet, information about Amalie had eluded him.

Her glassware shop, Bohemian Delights, was known throughout Prague as one of the best places to source both antique crystal and modern pieces in all of Europe. Add to her varied inventory her immense knowledge about her products, and it would be foolish to purchase crystal elsewhere, which, he imagined, made her business quite lucrative. Compounding the mystery was that her shop made almost all of its sales after dark.

In fact, the shop was rarely open during the day. In a tourist haven such as Prague, not being open during regular hours would mean missing the crush of bodies that regularly plagued Old Town, searching for souvenirs like *pisankas* with their names painted on the side. But if you craved a consultation with Amalie, the expert herself, those only happened at night.

Why is that, Hawk wondered.

Hawk also preferred living at night. He never got out of bed before sunset if it could be helped, and was typically back between the sheets with a partner or two long before sunrise. His nocturnal habits were what drove him to the entertainment industry. With night clubs and bars as his focus, he could sink his time and expertise into a business that matched his lifestyle. Hawk often wondered what people like him had done in times past, when evening activities were lit by candlelight instead of electricity.

Actually, he would quite enjoy conducting business by candlelight.

Hawk was ruminating on opening a new candlelight-only club, and wondering how he could manage to stay within the city's strict fire regulations, when the bouncer, Henri, elbowed him. Hawk followed his gaze, and lost his breath.

Amalie was walking down the cobbled street, her gazed fixed on him; he noticed she was limping, favoring her left leg. Even with the limp, she didn't appear weak. If anything, she resembled a warrior returning from battle, scarred but victorious.

Aside from her gait, Amalie was a true vision of beauty. She was wearing a blue silk dress, and the thin fabric hugged her curves and accentuated every graceful movement she made. Her décolletage was as modest as the skirt's side slit was daring, reaching her upper thigh. Amalie had left her dark hair loose, and it rippled down her back. She wore no jewelry, but with her onyx eyes and ruby lips she didn't need to.

When Amalie reached the club, she tilted her chin up, and said, "Hello, Hawk."

Hawk smiled. "You came."

Her black eyes flashed. "Not yet."

He laughed, since he hadn't expected her to flirt with him so blatantly, then he offered her his arm. "My lady, if you will?"

Amalie accepted his arm, and he led her inside. "I must ask, why have you named this establishment the Moravian Ballroom?"

The corner of Hawk's mouth curled up. He liked that she was interested in his business. That meant she was interested in him. "I am Moravian," he replied. "My family hails from Ostrava. As for the other part of the name, that honors my mother. She was a dance instructor."

"Was she?" They stepped onto a balcony that overlooked the dance floor below. Hundreds of people moved in time to the ear-splitting music, the lot of them illuminated by a rainbow of stage lights. "What would she think of this spectacle you've created?"

Hawk looked around his club, first at the tall mirrors behind the bar, to the enormous state of the art DJ booth, to his many happy patrons. "She would love it."

"Then you have done well. All good boys look to please their mother," she added.

Hawk dipped his chin. "A fine compliment. Come, let's get you a drink."

"I doubt you have what I like."

"We have everything." When Hawk felt her fingers tense on his arm, he added, "On the off chance we're found wanting, I'll send someone to get whatever you desire."

"Anything?"

"Anything." They entered a private alcove, and Hawk watched her slide into the circular, padded booth. "Well? What exotic beverage would please you?"

"I'm curious to see what you offer me."

Hawk grinned; while he'd long sought to know his neighbor, he never thought he'd have this much fun with her. He whispered a few instructions to the server, then he joined Amalie in the booth.

"What did you order?"

"Patience, Nightingale."

Her eyes narrowed. "Again, with that name. It's not like you've ever heard me sing."

"I've heard you many times," he replied. "When I first inspected this property, back when it was nothing more than a drafty old warehouse, your voice wafted through the walls. I asked the realtor who was singing in a warehouse near midnight, and he answered that it could only be Amalie Vyrdolak, the most famous shopkeeper in Old Town."

"I doubt anyone thinks I'm famous," she demurred. "Why were you inspecting this place at midnight? Surely you could see more of it in the daylight."

"I prefer to conduct my business at night. I find that with the proper amount of persuasion, most will accommodate me."

Before Hawk could continue two servers arrived, and set out two martinis, four glasses of wine—two red, two white—a crystal decanter of whiskey with matching glasses, and an ice bucket with a bottle of champagne chilling inside. "Will there be anything else, sir?" one of the servers asked.

"This is perfect. Thank you."

The servers left with their empty trays, and Amalie faced Hawk. "I see your plan is to get me drunk."

"My plan is to offer you the best of what we have," he corrected. "I trust something here is to your liking?"

Amalie crossed her legs, the slit in her dress exposing one nearly to her waist. "And if I desire something else?"

Hawk moved closer to her. "Such as?"

Amalie ran a finger down the column of his throat, and said, "What I desire is pleasure." Then, she bit him.

Hawk sat straight up in bed. He had no memory of returning home from the club, his muscles ached, and he was naked. That last bit wasn't unusual, but he couldn't shake the feeling that something had happened. Something important.

He ran a hand through his hair, and felt wetness on his neck. He looked at his hand. His fingers were stained red.

Hawk stared at the blood on his hand, wondering if he'd gotten into a fight at the club. As he turned his hand back and forth to inspect the blood, his cock hardened; odd, since blood wasn't one of his usual kinks. He drew the sheet aside to admire his member, and found two small puncture wounds on the inside of his thigh.

Bite marks.

"What the fuck," he muttered. He could forgive himself a bit of memory loss over a fight or other accident, but whatever had bitten him had been a hair's breadth from his balls. Wondering what he'd had to drink to make him forget this near-castration, Hawk retraced his steps from the night before. He remembered opening the club, reserving a private booth, then waiting for...

Amalie.

Chapter Three

Amalie - Prague,
Present Day

Amalie opened up the large cabinet in the back of the main room of her shop, and began cleaning the most delicate items she carried. It was a ritual she performed weekly, whether the dust had accumulated or not, and one she always completed alone. She'd had some of the pieces for decades, and a few since before she was turned. Still others she'd made herself. Amalie still remembered the glassblower she'd worked for in Murano, and how he'd taught her a few tricks. Some of those tricks had even involved glassware.

She moved a filigree egg aside and saw her garnet. It lay in the very back of the case on a simple stand, a humble place for so great a gem. It was an oval shape and polished to a mirror sheen; most who saw it assumed it was a lump of colored glass, due to its large size and flawless construction. But it was the real thing, and Amalie remembered when the garnet used to rest at the hollow of her throat every day and night.

Especially every night.

She also remembered the throat she'd ripped it off of, thus earning her the title of clan mistress, along with a lifelong enemy. She hadn't wanted to run afoul of Marek or his clan, but once he'd lost her trust, and then her heart, she'd had no choice. And that was why the garnet that proclaimed her leader of her clan and his was kept in her shop, behind bullet-proof glass and watched by surveillance cameras, rather than in her home. Eventually, Marek would come for it, and Amalie wanted to be ready.

When Marek came—because it was certainly a when, not an if—Amalie only hoped she could save as many of her people as possible.

The door chime sounded behind her. Before Amalie could turn around or close the cabinet, a man yelled, "You're sick!"

Amalie smiled, having recognized Hawk's voice. "Am I?" she asked as she faced him. Unlike the refined, perfectly dressed man she'd spent the prior evening with at the Moravian Ballroom, today's Hawk was disheveled and wild-eyed.

"You bit me," he ground out.

"You liked it." She approached Hawk, and looked pointedly at the marks on his neck. "As I recall, you liked it quite a bit."

"How did I get home?" he demanded. "Who put me in my bed?"

Amalie cocked her head to the side; she hadn't realized he'd never been bitten before. "Was last night your first time? I thought you were more worldly than that." When his pale eyes flashed, she continued, "For many, the first time they're bitten, the pleasure is so intense it causes a bit of amnesia. Your memories will return, in time."

Hawk closed the distance between them, standing so close she had to tilt her head back to maintain eye contact. "Did we fuck?"

She placed her hand on his chest. "We did not, but you came. Several times, in fact."

He blinked. "Next time, I want to remember everything," he said, then he kissed her. Amalie had expected him to crush his mouth against hers as he'd done last night at the club, but he was gentle. Tender, even, as his tongue stroked her lips. With a sigh, they parted for him. A moment later he found her fangs, and he lightly scraped his tongue against the delicate points.

"Seeing if it was real?" Amalie asked when they parted.

"Seeing if I'm crazy." He stroked her hair, and then her neck. "You could have told me."

"Those conversations don't always go well, but you're right," she admitted, feeling a pang of guilt. "I should have told you. Forgive me?"

"Only if you promise to come back to my club tonight."

"You grant your forgiveness so easily?"

He tucked a loose strand of hair behind her ear. "I was more embarrassed than mad, and I shouldn't have yelled like a madman in your shop. I suppose, since we've both misbehaved, now we're even."

Laughter bubbled up from her throat. "If you think a bite is equal to a bit of yelling, you really do have amnesia." She sobered, and added, "I am sorry for not telling you. After the first bite, you went along with everything so willingly, I assumed you would remember."

"Come to my club tonight, and we can make new memories."

"Would it be all right if I came earlier?" she asked. "The music was distracting, and I wish to give you my full attention."

"Sunset then?" he asked, and she smiled. He paused, and asked, "Do you like to drink things other than blood, or did I waste hundreds of dollars' worth of product, too?"

Amalie laughed. "We drank the red wine, and the champagne," she replied. "I'm not a fan of whiskey, though, so that went untouched, as did the martinis. Forgive me?"

Hawk kissed her knuckles. "Forgiven, my nightingale. I will be waiting for you."

With that, Hawk swept out of Amalie's shop with a grace and dignity that belied her memory of him on his knees, begging for more bites. Amalie watched him disappear down the street, and briefly contemplating following him. But she assumed he was busy, and she did have several tasks of her own to complete before sunset. When she turned back to her display case, Iveta was scowling at her.

"You *bit* him?" she demanded. "You, the woman who insisted we could not attract that buffoon's notice, bit him?"

Amalie pursed her lips as she gathered up her cleaning supplies. "It wasn't something I planned on doing," she began. "But he was so kind at the club—"

"The club? You bit him in public?" Iveta screeched. "Amalie, this is a dangerous game you're playing. What if someone saw you?"

"Hawk's people are loyal to him." It had been plain that Hawk treated his employees well, which made them both attentive and discreet. "They would not betray him."

"Not unless they were also loyal to *him*." Out of long habit Iveta refrained from mentioning the name of Amalie's once-husband, the warlord Marek. There were ears everywhere, and many of those ears belonged to Marek. Iveta took Amalie's hands, and said, "I have protected you for too long, against too many threats, to let a mortal unravel it all now. Please, my lady, be careful."

"I will." When Iveta raised her eyebrows, Amalie laughed. "I will be careful. Promise."

Iveta squeezed her hands. "See that you are."

Chapter Four

Amalie - Prussian Village, Before

THE DAY AFTER AMALIE'S sixteenth birthday, word came to her village about Marek's impending arrival so he could collect the tithe. The warlord hadn't been through that area of Europe in so long no one living had been to a tithe, but the memories lingered. As Amalie soon learned, memories of such events lingered long after death.

When Marek's entourage arrived in the village square, the elders wasted no time in making him feel welcome. Bonfires were lit and larders were emptied, for while her village was small, it had never lacked for resources. The elders spared no expense, and Amalie wondered why this soldier was being feted like a king. Her friend Katia took her aside, and explained the tithe, and the man who collected it.

"Do you not know, Ama?" Katia asked. "The Marek is *upyr*."

Upyr. Vampire. Intrigued, Amalie looked toward the long tables where the Marek and his men were seated. "Which one is he?"

Katia pointed to a man near the center of the table. "Him," she whispered.

"He's handsome," Amalie said. Marek wore a bear pelt across his shoulders, fastened across his chest with a heavy gold chain that gleamed in the firelight. His hair and eyes were almost dark as Amalie's, and he was easily the most attractive man she'd ever seen. Next to him sat a woman with hair as pale as straw, wearing an emerald green cloak and a large garnet at her throat.

"Who's that next to him?" Amalie asked. "His wife?"

"His mother, Varushka," Katia replied. "Marek is the warlord, but she is the true leader of the clan."

"Then he does not have a wife," Amalie mused.

"What are you thinking?" Katia asked, then she saw how her friend's eyes tracked Marek's every move. "Ama, no," Katia said, shaking her head. "Those who leave with him never return!"

"Why would I ever want to return to this place?" Amalie asked. What she wanted was to no longer be an orphaned peasant, struggling just to feed herself. She wanted to be a rich man's wife, and if she married a feared and handsome man like Marek she would feel like a queen. "There is nothing for me here. There hasn't been, not since my parents died."

Katia frowned, but didn't argue. "Look at the elders," she said. "They're already negotiating the tithe with his advisors. You may get your wish whether you like it or not, Ama."

"Why?" she asked. "What is the tithe?" Ever since her parents had passed, precious little news reached her. As a ward of the village her only uses had been mending shirts and peeling vegetables, and the elders didn't share secrets with seamstresses or cooks. As for her voice, which was equal in strength as clarity as her mother's was, she was rarely given the opportunity to sing. That honor went to the elders' wives.

"The tithe is flesh," Katia whispered. "Whenever he comes to feast, all of the unmarried women are lined up for his pleasure. He takes whomever he likes, sometimes for a night, and sometimes forever."

"Forever," Amalie murmured. There was nothing for her in the village, save for a loveless marriage to either an old widower, where she would care for the house and children as more of a servant than wife, or a lowly member of society such as a stable hand or muckraker. Amalie didn't want to spend her days and nights scrubbing and toiling and smelling like shit. She wanted to be powerful, admired, envied.

She wanted Marek to choose her.

Having come to an agreement with the warlord's men, the elders began dragging women from the edge of the square to the center, and arranging them into a line in front of the feasting table. Amalie noticed that she wasn't the only one who went willingly, and struggled to place herself directly in front of Marek. She ended up a bit to his left, but close enough for her to see the fine gold embroidery on his velvet sleeves. Close enough for him to see her.

Not that he was looking in her direction. The elders were at the far end of the line from Amalie, taking their time as they presented each woman to the warlord, reciting each's name and talents in turn. Amalie hated waiting, but she would hate being pulled out of the line even more. She thrust her hands into the folds of her skirts, and tried to be patient.

Finally, the old men got to her, and Father Micah simply said, "This is Amalie."

Amalie smiled and curtsied at Marek, then the old men moved on to the next woman. Frantic that her one chance to leave her village was slipping away, she pulled open her bodice and bared herself to the waist.

"My lord," she called. Marek's gaze returned to her. He smiled as the villagers gasped and called her names; witch, harlot, Amalie had heard them all. The other women in line craned their necks to see what she'd done to get the warlord's attention. To Amalie's dismay others began baring themselves as well.

"We should come here more often," Marek said as his gaze swept across the line of half-dressed women. "This is the most beautiful village I've ever seen!"

Marek's soldiers laughed and leered, and Amalie did the only thing she could. She sang.

"Who is that?" Marek held up a hand, silencing his soldiers. He pointed at Amalie. "Step forward." She did, being sure to leave her dress open. "Sing."

Amalie did, and she sang of the moon, and the stars, and the icy beauty of the spring snowmelt, and the lush warmth of being wrapped in furs as the winter winds howled outside. She sang of love, and death, and beauty, all the while her gaze never leaving Marek's. When her song was done, Marek's gaze darkened.

"Your voice is beautiful," he said. "Easily as beautiful as your form. Who taught you to sing like a nightingale?"

"My mother," she replied. "She was the *cantata* for this village."

Marek nodded. "You're leaving with me. Tonight."

Amalie smiled. "As you wish, my lord."

Chapter Five

Hawk -Prague,
Present Day

Shortly before sunset Hawk stood beside the club's front entrance, once again waiting for Amalie's arrival. As he stood next to Henri, he consider his behavior. He hadn't waited on a lover with such impatience since he was a teenager, but now he could think about nothing but Amalie's black eyes and her deep red lips.

Red with my blood, no doubt. Once he'd gotten over the initial shock of having been bitten, he didn't mind that she was a vampire. Now, he was intrigued. He'd heard many stories about vampires, and was interested to separate fact from fiction. Maybe he would feed her some garlic bread, or walk her past a few mirrors, just to see what would happen.

He'd already learned that the myth of feeling profound pleasure from their bite was, in fact, one hundred percent true. While his memory of the previous evening was still hazy, whenever he thought about Amalie his skin thrummed with pleasure. Hawk's body remembered the evening they'd shared, even if his mind didn't.

Something else he'd heard about vampires was that regularly ingesting their victim's blood healed them, and kept their youthful appearance intact. Amalie looked to be no older that thirty, but now Hawk wondered how old she really was. One hundred, maybe, or perhaps she'd seen one thousand years? More than one thousand years, even?

Hawk shook his head. Taut unlined skin was one thing, but immortality was beyond what he could accept. Besides, if Amalie was hundreds or thousands of years old, wouldn't she speak or act like an elder? If anything, she beheld the world around her with wonder, not the jaded gaze of someone who had already seen and done it all. Add to that how Amalie favored her left leg, and Hawk suspected many of the stories were just that, stories.

He couldn't wait to discover the truth.

Henri cleared his throat, and jerked his chin toward the street. Hawk followed his gaze, and saw Amalie.

His Amalie.

There's another myth disproven. Amalie was once again coming toward him, the slanting rays of the setting sun bathing her in golden light. As she'd done the night before she wore a thin silk sheath that did little to hide her body, though this one was black instead of last evening's jewel toned blue. Her shoes were matching black slippers—he noted that she was careful on the cobbled street, placing her feet deliberately—and her only jewelry was a large oval garnet that rested in the hollow her throat.

"Where did you find her, and does she have a sister?" Henri asked.

Hawk chuckled. "If anything, she found me. I'll ask about siblings." He stepped away from the building and offered Amalie a shallow bow. "My nightingale."

Amalie smiled. "Such poise," she said, as she accepted his hand. "Have you reserved another table for us?"

"I have, but this one is in a private room." He glanced at her, and added, "I thought it best, in case you get me naked again."

"You took your clothes off of your own accord," Amalie said, as Henri choked down a laugh. "I merely enjoyed the show."

Hawk glared good naturedly at Henri, then he led Amalie inside the club. Thanks to the early hour, the music's volume was kept to a dull roar, and only a few patrons sat at the bar. "As you can see, we do very little business during the day."

"Is it profitable for you to remain open during these hours?"

Hawk shrugged. "The nighttime crowd more than makes up for these sparse times. Besides, a few of the locals have made a habit of coming by in the afternoon, and as you know goodwill among the locals is everything to a business."

"It really is."

They went upstairs, and Hawk led Amalie into their private room for the evening. The front wall was floor to ceiling glass, where they could watch everything happening in the club below. A long countertop and stools ran the length of the window. At the back of the room was a couch, a small wet bar, and a few tables and chairs were set close to the wall.

"This is very nice," Amalie said. "Do you come up here often?"

"No, usually I'm in my office," he replied. "Before you ask, it's a small, windowless room, and it has barely enough room for my desk. It would be better used as a broom closet."

"Then, where do you keep the brooms?"

"In a larger space, actually."

Amalie smiled, then she leaned on the counter and swept her gaze across the club laid out beneath them. "Can we see your office from here?"

Hawk stood behind her, and set one hand on the counter next to her waist as the other came around her and indicated a hallway directly across the way from their vantage point. "It's there, second door from the left. Planning how to surprise attack me?"

"Perhaps." She leaned back against him. "I really am sorry about last night. I didn't realize you'd never been bitten, or would forget what happened. That's not how I wanted things to begin between us."

"It's all right. You said my memories will return in time, and I believe you." He moved her hair from the side of her neck, and caressed her pale skin. "If you keep biting me, will I become a vampire?"

She laughed softly. "No. There's more to it than that."

"Good to know." He continued stroking her neck, and smiled when she shivered. "How many times did you bite me?"

"Three. Twice on the neck, and once a bit lower."

Remembering the marks on his inner thigh, his smile widened. "I know how I can truly forgive you. Let me kiss your skin in every place where you've bitten me."

"Every place?"

"Every place."

Amalie turned around and pressed herself against his chest. "What of your pristine glass? I thought you were a voyeur, not an exhibitionist," she added.

"This is two way glass," he said, as his head dipped lower and he nuzzled her neck. "This side is clear, but the side that faces the club is a mirror. No one will see you but me, my nightingale."

"In that case," she began, then she slid the straps of her dress off her shoulders and let the silk fall, baring herself to her waist. "I think your idea is brilliant."

Hawk lifted her onto the counter and kissed a path from her neck to her breasts. Amalie unbuttoned his shirt and unfastened his belt, pausing to moan when he sucked the tip of her breast between his teeth.

"Will you sing for me, my nightingale?"

"Yes, my Hawk. I will sing for you."

Later, Hawk lounged on the couch, completely naked and perfectly relaxed with his legs stretched out in front of him and an arm propped behind his head. He watched as Amalie, her smooth skin bare as well, moved behind the bar. She poured two glasses of red wine, and joined him on the couch.

"May I ask you something?" she asked, as she passed him a glass.

"Of course."

"Why are you called The Hawk?"

He laughed softly. "The reason isn't remotely interesting. My name is Jonathan Hawker."

"How can you say that isn't interesting?" She traced her finger across his forearm. "I like learning about you."

"Do you? I'd like to learn about you, too."

"Please. I'm sure you have many questions."

Hawk set his glass aside, and took Amalie's hand. "I saw you walking in sunlight. It doesn't burn you."

"My skin is very sensitive, and I will have a nasty burn if I remain in the sun for too long, but it's not like the movies. I won't turn into a pile of ash. If I was a newer vampire, it would be different." She hid a smile behind her wineglass, and added, "Were you planning on feeding me garlic just to see what would happen?"

"Never," he replied, hoping he hadn't said his earlier comment about garlic bread out loud. "Have you been a vampire for a long time? Wait, is vampire the politically correct term? Person of blood, perhaps?"

"Vampire is correct," she replied. "As for how long I have been this way, when I came of age my clan gave me to a vampire warlord as a payment for his continued protection. He collected a tithe every time he passed through the village, and that year the payment was me. I stood next to his throne and sang for him for many, many years. He liked my voice so much he made me like him, so he would never be without my songs. Then, he made me his queen."

Hawk almost choked on his wine. "You're married to a warlord?"

"Was," she corrected. "We had a good run, then our disagreements outnumbered our happinesses, and I led a revolt against him. This," she indicated the garnet at her throat, "marks me as the clan leader."

Hawk stroked the skin below her necklace. "Did you rip this bauble from his throat?"

"His mother's, actually."

"And now you run a shop selling trinkets to tourists." Hawk shook his head. "Your life has taken some turns, my nightingale."

"And you run a club where you fuck vampires in the back room," Amalie countered.

"Vampire," he corrected. "You are the only one allowed to bite me."

"Loyalty is a very attractive trait." Amalie set her wineglass aside, and Hawk saw a pale web of scars on the curve of her left hip.

"How did this happen?" he asked, as he stroked the scars. They were so long healed there were little more than silver streaks meandering from her waist downward.

"The warlord I mentioned? We had an altercation." She nestled herself against his side, and stroked the top of his thigh. "He made plans to turn me, but his mother was not pleased. She thought I was a bad influence on him, and thought if I was turned it would be increased tenfold. So, she set my bed on fire."

"With you in it?"

"Oh, yes. It was quite the spectacle. Screaming, crying, all of it."

"Did he turn you to save you?"

She laughed softly. "No. He turned me because he wanted to own me."

"Then he was a fool," Hawk declared. "No one owns you. If he'd ever truly seen you, he would have known that."

"You think so?" Amalie asked, as she straddled Hawk's body.

"I'm certain of it." He gently squeezed her hip. "Does it still hurt?"

"No. Those wounds healed a very long time ago." She dragged her finger from his throat to his navel. "You're the first mortal I've bitten in a very long time."

"You're loyal as well, then?" Hawk cupped her bottom, and guided his cock to her entrance.

"I aim to be." Amalie kissed him, scraping her fangs across his lower lip and she slid onto him. Hawk tensed, the twin pleasures in his mouth and his cock threatening to make him black out again. He gripped Amalie's hips as he forced her to slow down, forced his mind to remain clear.

"Hawk?" she asked, as she raised her head. "What's wrong?"

"I don't want to forget," he rasped.

She stroked his hair back from his forehead, and began to move her hips in a slow rhythm. "If you do, I will help you remember."

Chapter Six

Amalie - Marek's Camp, Before

AFTER THE NOVELTY OF sleeping with the warlord wore off, Amalie was once again bored with her daily life. Since she remained human, she was assigned some of the camp's chores such as seeing to the laundry and food preparation. The work wasn't nearly as difficult as what she'd endured in her village, but Amalie had not given her body to a vampire to become a washerwoman or a potato peeler. She wanted more.

Adding to her dissatisfaction was the way the human cattle were treated. Many of Marek's soldiers viewed the humans as little more than walking meals, though Amalie was excluded from that aspect. Only Marek fed from her, or, on occasion, his mother, Varushka. Amalie shuddered, her skin crawling with the memory of the last time she'd been invited—or rather, ordered—into the vampire queen's bed. Varushka bit down just a little too hard, and left her fangs in Amalie's flesh just a little too long. Amalie suspected that the only thing keeping her alive was her status as Marek's favorite. Once that changed, Varushka would eat her for dinner. Literally.

As if to confirm her fears, Amalie regularly saw humans carried out of Varushka's bedchamber, some so drained of blood they were grey and cold. Once, the cleaners had dropped a man's corpse and it shattered on the floor; Varushka had drained him so completely he'd been rendered to a husk.

Then came the night Amalie's friend, Katia, had gone into Varushka's room. She never came out.

"But why do you go through so many?" Amalie asked one night, as she lay in Marek's bed. The best time to ask him questions was in bed, when he was lazy and sated on both blood and sex.

"Sometimes we can't help ourselves," Marek said. "Especially the newer soldiers who don't get to feed as often. The hunger overtakes them. Besides, there are always more humans."

"But what—"

"Amalie." Marek's hand closed over her throat. "I am not going to spare the humans, no matter how many ways you fuck me."

"I don't want you to spare them," Amalie said, careful to remain still. Marek's nails were as sharp as his fangs, and she'd witness him rip out at least a score of throats. "I only worry that your supply could run low, and you might have to share me." Amalie pressed her body against his. "I only like the way you taste me. The others are so rough. And," she continued, tracing a fingertip down his chest, "I know you don't like to share."

Marek laughed, and Amalie let herself breathe again. She never knew if he would find her alluring or annoying, and the latter could mean death. "You're right, my songstress. I do want to keep you all for myself. What would you have me do?"

"Maybe let the younglings feed more often," she suggested; controlling a new vampire's blood supply was one of many ways Marek exerted control over his clan. "Not much more often, since they still need to learn their place. Just a few drops here and there, so those brutes don't destroy their food." She climbed on top of him, and said, "Dogs play with their food, but you, my lover, are raising wolves."

Marek laughed again, his hands clutching Amalie's hips. His talons dug into her flesh, but Amalie didn't wince or cry out. Showing weakness to Marek was akin to begging for death. "Very well, my beauty, a little more food for all. Perhaps it will make my soldiers love me all the more."

Amalie leaned forward until her neck was against his mouth, and let him sink his fangs into her throat. "Of course they will, my lover."

The next day, two guards yanked Amalie out of her bed and hauled her into Varushka's chamber. "You told my son to feed the younglings more?" the vampire demanded.

"I asked him to allow them a few drops here and there so they wouldn't drain the cattle all at once," Amalie shot back. "If they use up all the cattle the favorites will be next, and I do not want to be their dinner."

Varushka ran a finger along Amalie's jaw, and tilted her head to the side, exposing her neck. "You think you're too good to feed my soldiers?"

"I'm not. But I am terrified of what they'll do to me." Amalie swallowed, watching as Varushka's gaze tracked her throat's movements. "I am far more terrified of you."

"You should be." Varushka tugged open Amalie's shift and pinched her nipple. Amalie gasped at the sudden pain, since Varushka's talons were as sharp as Marek's. "Did that hurt, little one?"

"Y-Yes."

Varushka licked Amalie's blood from her thumb. "Do you think being given to the younglings would be more painful?"

"Yes, my lady."

"Can you think of anything that might be more painful?"

"I'm not sure," Amalie replied. "Perhaps a whipping?"

Varushka grinned, and Amalie realized her mistake. "Excellent idea, my pet. I'll have you whipped, and then you need never suffer one of my soldiers."

"No, my lady," Amalie fell to her knees and clasped her hands in front of her heart. "Please, Varushka, I will do anything for you, but please don't whip me."

"You would rather feed my soldiers?" When Amalie didn't answer, Varushka nodded to her guards. "Take off her dress, and march her to the front of the tent."

And so Amalie was stripped and led through the mass of vampires to the whipping post at the front of the main tent. As she walked through the crowd the others raked their hands and gazes across her skin, with some even licking the trail of blood that dripped from her breast. When she reached the platform, Marek extended his hand.

"Really, songstress, you brought this upon yourself," he said. She nodded, and didn't flinch as he raised her arms high overhead, or as he tightened the rope around her wrists. Once he deemed her properly secure, Marek leaned close to her ear, and murmured, "If I take it too far, I may have to turn you. I'd hate to let you die, and never hear you sing again."

"Do what you must, my lord."

Marek raised the whip, and began lashing her back to the cheers of the crowd. He didn't limit his punishment to her back, and the whip bit into her thighs and calves, and even her feet. As the crowd chanted for more carnage, more blood, Amalie felt her soul loosen from her body. She didn't allow it to leave her body, even though she desperately wanted the pain to end. Instead, she began to plot her revenge.

Chapter Seven

Amalie - Prague, Present Day

Amalie walked home early the next morning, her shoes dangling from her hand as she enjoyed the sunlight on her skin. Despite her nocturnal nature she'd always enjoyed the sun. When Marek had first turned her, and her new immortal skin became too delicate to withstand the sun's rays, she'd cried for days. He'd assured her that, in time, her skin would adjust and she would be able to walk in the daylight once again. It had taken decades, but it had come to pass. If only Marek had been as truthful about other things he'd told her.

A chill rolled down her spine, and she gathered Hawk's coat close about her. Her mortal man had been so gracious as she was leaving, asking her to stay with him for the rest of the day or at least for breakfast, and offering her his coat when she declined both invitations. Truth be told she would love to spend a day or three in bed with him, but she had much to do. Her clan, and her shop, left her little free time.

Even though Amalie craved a hot bath and a few hours of sleep, she went to her shop before she returned to her home. She still had the garnet on her, and wanted to return it to the safety of the reinforced cabinet as soon as possible. When she approached the front door, she saw something black and shiny lying across the threshold. When she realized what it was, she swore.

It was a dead raven, Marek's ham fisted yet effective calling card. She knew without checking the bird had been strangled; it was his preferred method of execution. He'd strangled her many times, just to prove he could. Amalie knelt next to the raven, and touched its feathers.

"I'm so sorry, little friend," she said. "Fly free in the next world."

Amalie withdrew her keys, intending to go inside and find a length of cloth to wrap up the bird, and found the door already unlocked. She dropped her keys into her pocket, and pushed the door open. The lights were off, but that didn't matter. Her vision was excellent, as was her hearing, and neither were affected by darkness. As she scanned the front room of her shop, she heard movement near the ceiling. Amalie spun around to face the noise as Iveta dropped down from the rafters.

"What happened?" Amalie demanded.

"Two of Marek's people came looking for you," Iveta replied. "They're dead."

Amalie spied the spray of blood across Iveta's breast and face. "Are you hurt?"

"This isn't my blood," Iveta scoffed. "Marek must be desperate. He sent younglings after me, and they didn't last more than five minutes."

"It was a test," Amalie said. "He sent the most expendable people he had. When they don't return by sunset, he'll know you still guard me."

"Was I supposed to let them live?"

"Of course not," Amalie said. "You did the right thing, as you have always done. I, on the other hand, am a fool." Amalie opened her coat, and revealed the garnet.

"You wore it when you went to see your mortal?" Iveta shook her head, and found a rag to wipe the blood from her face. "This man means so much to you?"

Amalie pursed her lips. "I hadn't considered why I was wearing it. I put it on almost as an afterthought." She glanced at Iveta's bloody shirt, and covered her face with her hands. "And because of my afterthought, you were forced to kill again, two younglings are dead, and Marek knows where we are."

"No one has ever forced me to do anything," Iveta said, as she grasped Amalie's hands and lowered them from her face. "I chose to follow you all those years ago, and choose to follow you now. I defend your body with my own, and you in turn keep the clan safe, and hidden."

Amalie smiled; no one knew the names and locations of every clan member, save her and Iveta. "We wouldn't have lasted this long without you."

"Remember that. As for the younglings, they also made their choices," Iveta continued. "They were responsible for their fates, no one else."

"And Marek?" Amalie prompted.

"Marek has probably known where we are all along." Iveta stepped back, and pulled her ruined shirt up and over her head. "He's always relied more on spies than warriors, which is another reason why those younglings didn't last long."

"I always told him he should be more careful with his people," Amalie muttered. "Come, I'll help you get cleaned up. Then, we must alert our own warriors. I refuse to lose anyone else to Marek."

Iveta nodded. "We've lost enough already. It's time for him to know how it feels."

After a hot bath and a hearty breakfast, Amalie was ready to face her treacherous ex-lover. It was Marek's way to lurk in the shadows and wait for her to exhibit the barest shred of happiness before lashing out at her. Why go after a lonely shopkeeper, when he could wait for her to find a new, better lover, and then pull the rug out from under her feet. And why did Marek know Amalie had a new lover? Because she went prancing around Prague wearing scandalous dresses while wearing the garnet.

"Arrogance and stupidity," Amalie spat, her anger at herself making her blood boil. How could she have been so foolish? Wearing the garnet in public was sure to attract attention, and she'd been so careful for so many years. Then Hawk strode into her shop, and she felt an attraction to him that she hadn't felt to anyone in years. If she were a younger woman, she would call it love at first sight.

But Amalie wasn't a young woman. She was an old, old vampire, the head of her small clan, and had once been the consort to one of the deadliest undead warlords in history. She knew better than to call her new interest in Hawk anything other than an infatuation, regardless of whether or not it was mutual. In fact, it hardly mattered if it was mutual, because in a few decades Hawk would be gone, and Amalie would still remain.

That is, unless Marek managed to kill her this time. Then Hawk would live on long after her demise.

I refuse to let that bastard win.

She also refused to leave Hawk in the dark. Most vampires thought mortals beneath their notice, and that granted Hawk a modicum of safety from Marek's plans. However, she needed to tell Hawk that she may have inadvertently compromised both him and his club. If anything happened to Hawk, or one of his people, she would never forgive herself.

Amalie gritted her teeth, and dressed herself in jeans and a conservative sweater. She needed to speak with Hawk as soon as possible, and for once she couldn't let sex get in the way. After what she told him, Hawk would probably never want to see her again.

A short time later, Amalie stood on Hawk's front step working up the nerve to knock on his door. She didn't know if he was home, or even awake, but this awful news was the sort of information best delivered in person. That way, he could look her in the eye when he called her a monster and cursed the day they met.

Cowardice is the least sexy trait. She took a breath, and knocked. Less than a minute later, Hawk himself opened the door.

"Amalie," he said, surprised but not offended by her impromptu visit. "I wasn't expecting to see you again so soon, but I'm happy you're here."

"I'm sorry for the intrusion, but something has happened."

"You are not intruding." He stepped aside, and beckoned her to enter. "Please, come in."

Amalie entered, and rounded on Hawk as soon as he closed the door. "I'm so sorry, but an old enemy of mine had learned of my location, and he may know of you, and your club."

Hawk ran a hand through his hair. "I've just made some coffee. Let's go to the kitchen, and talk."

"We can't sit around having coffee when such things are in motion!"

"I can." When Amalie frowned, he added, "I do my best thinking after coffee. Come, indulge my simple mortal ways."

He smiled and held out his hand, and Amalie's heart softened. "All right, but this is business, not a breakfast date."

"Who said anything about breakfast? You expect me to feed you, too?" Despite his words, as soon as Amalie was seated in one of the tall bar stools at the kitchen counter Hawk poured her a cup of coffee, then he began laying out an assortment of fruit and pastries.

"I thought you lived alone," she said. "Why do you keep so much food on hand?"

"My employees frequently come here before and after their shifts," he explained. "They're often hungry, so I feed them."

"You're very good to your people."

"They work hard, and I appreciate them." Hawk sat across from her. "Tell me what's wrong."

"What isn't wrong," she began, and told him how she had once used her nightingale's voice to attract the attention of Marek, the most ruthless vampire warlord in Eastern Europe. The village elders had used her voice and her body to pay that year's tithe, and Amalie had gone willingly.

Then she realized she would never be anything but Marek's slave.

She omitted the story of being tied to the whipping post, bare and bloody as Marek's people cheered for her death, but she did tell Hawk about being turned. After Amalie had gone to Marek's fangs she became his songstress and his consort, as close to a queen she could be while his mother, Varushka, still lived.

In Amalie's new role she was afforded unprecedented access to his world, and it wasn't long before she realized how evil he truly was, and how terrible he was to his people. Once Iveta had been given to Amalie as a handmaiden, and Marek turned her against her wishes, they began plotting his downfall in earnest. Her plan culminated in Marek's mother's death and Amalie's seizure of the garnet, an ancient symbol of the clan's power.

When she finished her tale, Hawk asked, "If that garnet is so precious, why did you wear it to my club?"

Amalie blinked; of all the questions she'd expected him to ask, it wasn't that. "I suppose I wanted to look nice for you."

Hawk took her hand, kissed her fingertips. "As always, you were beautiful."

"A moment of vanity and I may have doomed us all," Amalie said bitterly. "His people are already here. Marek left a dead raven across my shop's threshold, and Iveta killed two of his warriors last night."

"Iveta did that?" Hawk raised his eyebrows. "She is more than your assistant, isn't she?"

"Iveta has been with me for a very long time," Amalie replied. "After Marek turned me, he gave her to me as a toy, but I allowed her to train in secret as my bodyguard. When I led the revolt against Marek and Varushka, she was my first supporter. She has placed herself between me and danger at every turn. I don't know what I would do without her."

Hawk nodded. "As fierce as you and Iveta are, you two cannot go against this Marek alone. How can I help?"

"You cannot help," Amalie said. "It's too dangerous, and this isn't your fight."

"Isn't it? If I hadn't built my club so close to your shop, the music wouldn't have broken your wares. If I hadn't gone to your shop in person and demanded you come to the club, you never would have set foot there. And, if I hadn't been so enticingly bitable, you wouldn't have retuned a second time wearing the garnet." He took Amalie's hand, and studied her fingertips. "It seems that we're in this situation together, my nightingale."

Amalie curled her fingers against Hawk's. "Heaven help us all."

CHAPTER EIGHT

HAWK - PRAGUE,
PRESENT DAY

THEY SPENT A FEW more hours in the kitchen while Hawk cooked and Amalie ate almost everything he offered her; she shared that she'd never been a fan of fried sausages or bacon, but she devoured the omelet filled with cheese and sprinkled with chives. While he learned more about his nightingale's likes and dislikes, Hawk was also trying to convince Amalie to let him help her make a stand against this Marek.

"Where is the garnet now?" he asked. He was fascinated by the fact that a piece of jewelry could bestow the clan's leadership merely based on whoever wore it. Then again, he supposed crowns performed a similar function. Put one on your head and you not only looked like a monarch, you also appeared to be the most important person in the room.

"I have it on me." Amalie tugged down her sweater, and revealed the gem tucked inside her bra. "I should have been this discreet last night."

"Stop blaming yourself," he said. "If this Marek wants the garnet as badly as you say, he would have come for it eventually. Eventually just happened to be now." Hawk reached forward and tugged the collar of Amalie's sweater back into place, but paused when he noticed her staring at him.

"Forgive me," he said, as he withdrew his hands. "I didn't mean to overstep." Amalie caught his hands, and kissed his knuckles.

"One could argue that I overstepped first, by biting you without asking," she said.

"Fair point," Hawk said, then he pulled her to her feet. "I need to get to the club. If you're done eating all my food, I'll walk you home."

"You loved feeding me," she countered, and he didn't argue. "You don't know where I live."

"No, but there is a very nice house adjacent to your shop, and the locals say a beautiful woman is often seen in the windows, singing along with the birds," he said. "Either that's your house, or I'll meet someone new. Think this woman will bite me, too?"

Amalie swatted his arm, but she was laughing when she did so. When they reached the door, and Hawk grabbed an umbrella from the stand by the coat rack, she asked, "What's that for? It's not raining."

"It's to keep the sun off your skin. What, you want to fight Marek and deal with a sunburn at the same time?" Hawk opened the door and then the umbrella, then he extended his arm to Amalie. When she hesitated, he observed, "You're not used to letting others take care of you."

"I'm not," she said, and she relented and tucked her hand inside his elbow. "Usually I'm the one looking after the rest."

"Not even Iveta sees to your needs?"

A rather unladylike snort issued forth from Amalie's red lips. "Iveta's version of caring is committing a bloodless murder, so there's nothing for me to clean up afterwards."

"She's considerate. That's good." Hawk closed and locked the door behind them, then they started down the street. "It's too bad you're nocturnal. You're beautiful in the sunlight."

Amalie blushed and ducked her head, then something on the side of the street caught her eye. "What is it?" he asked, as he followed her gaze. There was a pile of black feathers on the side of the road.

"Odd." Hawk approached the feathers, and realized that someone had ripped a large black bird to pieces. "What sort of animal would have done this to a crow?"

"It's not a crow," Amalie said. "It's a raven."

"There's another," Hawk said, pointing to a second, larger pile of feathers.

"Hawk, get away!"

"What if we can save the birds?" he countered, then he realized what he was looking at. Next to the murdered raven was a hawk, its throat cut and the pale feathers on its breast matted with blood.

"Marek is here," Amalie said, her panicked gaze darting from one side of the street to the other. "Hawk, we need to run!"

CHAPTER NINE

AMALIE - PRAGUE,
PRESENT DAY

THEY RAN THROUGH THE narrow streets of Prague, dodging vendors as they shouted to each other and advertised their wares to the crowds. Amalie had no idea who in the city was working for Marek, which meant she assumed everyone but her and Hawk were on his payroll. Perhaps that was the wrong approach, but acting as though the entire world was against her had kept her alive this long. Hopefully it would work for a little longer.

"This way," Hawk said, and he pulled her into Old Town Square.

"Why are we stopping here," Amalie hissed, since they were exposed and vulnerable the center of the large courtyard. Hawk pressed a finger to his lips, and indicated the three tour groups reading pamphlets and listening as their guides regaled them with anecdotes of the city's history. Hawk approached one of the guides, and with a smile he accepted two of the pamphlets. He handed one to Amalie, and they joined a German sightseeing group.

"We will blend in here and take a moment to catch our breath, and decide what to do next," Hawk whispered, as the tour guide droned on about the astronomical clock. Amalie nodded, then faced the clock as it chimed the hour. The tourists *oohed* and *aahed* as the clock's ornate figures and planetary dials lurched into motion. Even though she'd watched the clock's show many times before, Amalie stood transfixed as the animatronic skeleton, which represented Death, struck the hour.

She wondered if this figure was a harbinger of sorts, and if Death was finally coming for her.

An explosion shook the ground. Hawk threw his arm around Amalie to steady her. "Earthquake?" he asked, as most of the crowd stumbled and fell to the ground around them.

"Look," Amalie said, and she pointed at a plume of smoke. "It's my shop," she said, and took off running toward the smoke. The streets were already choked with people running toward her as they fled to safety, but Amalie ignored them as she sprinted toward the smoke. She was faster than any mortal, and while she usually attempted to blend in with the common folk, now she tapped into her full speed.

Let them recognize her as a vampire. Let them try to catch her. Marek had never caught her. She doubted any mortal could. When she saw the remains of her shop, she gasped.

Both her shop and her adjacent home had been reduced to rubble.

"Iveta," Amalie yelled at the piles of rubble. "Iveta!"

Amalie launched herself at the remains of her livelihood, tossing aside chunks of concrete and stone and massive wooden beams as she searched for her dearest, oldest friend. On and on she dug, even as the dust caked her skin and made it difficult to breathe. Amalie had shifted most of the shop's remains when she found Iveta lying under what was left of the storeroom, unconscious but alive.

"Iveta," Amalie murmured, as she cradled her friend's limp form. "I'm so sorry, darling. I will make him pay for hurting you."

Hawk crouched beside her. "She's alive?"

"Yes. It takes a lot to kill one of us." Amalie was aware of the crowd of onlookers, murmuring in astonishment about how the petite shopkeeper had moved tons of rubble in under a minute. They could chalk it up to an adrenaline surge, or not for all Amalie cared. Iveta was alive, and Marek was going to pay.

Amalie heard whispers in the crowd behind her, talk of breached gas lines and faulty electrical wires having caused this disaster, but the only memories that played behind her eyes were of the time she returned to her home village and found every single home burned to the ground. Marek had burned them all because they had given him Amalie in the tithe, and after she'd betrayed him he went after everything she'd ever loved. Amalie hadn't loved her village, or the life she led before she became a vampire, but she never wanted to see anyone hurt. Marek had slaughtered every last mortal with even the most tenuous tie to her, all because he wanted her to feel nothing but pain.

I will hurt him, again and again if I have to. I will teach him what true pain feels like.

Amalie hissed at the crowd, baring her teeth as she dared them to take a step closer. She wasn't the scared country girl she once was. Now, she was a warlord in her own right.

"Amalie." Hawk set his hand on her shoulder. "We need to get off the street. Let me take her."

"I can carry her," Amalie protested.

"A small woman carrying an adult attracts attention," Hawk said. "The sort of attention we don't need."

He has a point. Amalie turned back to the crowd, saw how the women hid behind their men, and how the men frowned and clenched their fists. It was a scene she'd looked at too many times in her life, and she didn't have time to deal with a terrified mob. She needed to get Iveta somewhere safe so she could have time to heal.

Reluctantly, she let Hawk take Iveta's limp body. He lifted her against his shoulder, then he strode through the crowd and directly to the back door of his club, the one used for deliveries. Hawk kicked at the door, and a moment later Henri opened it.

"What the hell's going on?" Henri demanded. "It's like the end of the world out there." He saw Iveta's bloody face, and asked, "Is she going to be all right?"

"I hope so," Hawk replied. "The infirmary is stocked?"

"Always." Henri looked to Amalie. "Do you need anything?"

"Yes," Amalie said. "There's a man after us. After me. His name is Marek, and he will stop at nothing to get to me. Lock this door, and don't open it for anyone."

Henri glanced at Hawk, who nodded. Henri closed and locked the door, and watched as Hawk led Amalie to the club's infirmary.

"We keep this room stocked so we can deal with most small injuries on site," He said, as he laid Iveta on a cot pushed up against the wall. "On busy nights we employ a nurse." He opened his mouth, closed it.

"What?" Amalie asked, since he obviously wanted to say something.

"I was going to suggest calling the nurse in, but something tells me she won't be much help."

Despite everything, Amalie smiled. "You're very kind," she said, as she placed her hand on his jaw. He hadn't shaved that morning, and she liked the feel of his stubble. "And you're right, we are beyond what help mortal doctors can offer. I will heal Iveta myself."

"How?"

Amalie went to the medical cabinet, and found a scalpel. "With my blood."

CHAPTER TEN

HAWK - PRAGUE,
PRESENT DAY

HAWK LOOKED ON IN mingled horror and fascination as Amalie sliced her wrist open with the razor sharp scalpel, and pressed the dripping wound to Iveta's mouth. "Come, darling," Amalie murmured. "Drink for me. You need your strength."

"Your blood heals?" Hawk asked.

"It does," Amalie replied. "It can heal my kind, and yours as well." Iveta, roused by the blood, licked at Amalie's wrist, then she bit into the wound. Amalie swayed on her feet, and grabbed the wall with her free hand for support. Hawk rolled over a nearby chair and helped Amalie sit.

"What does this healing cost you?" he asked.

"I'll be weak for a time, but it will be worth it." Amalie withdrew her wrist from Iveta's mouth, and Hawk was ready with a roll of gauze to bind her wound. "If we're to face Marek, I'll need Iveta at her full strength."

"What else will you need?" Hawk asked as he bandaged Amalie's wrist. Once that was done, he dampened what was left of the gauze and cleaned Iveta's face.

"Need?" Amalie repeated. "An army, perhaps?"

"How can I help you?" Hawk amended. "Right now, what can I do for you?"

"I'll be fine." Amalie stood, only to lose her balance and steady herself against Hawk's chest. "Just give me a moment."

He scooped Amalie into his arms, and laid her on the cot next to Iveta. "Take all the time you need," he said, as he pulled a blanket over both of them. By the time he straightened up, Amalie had curled up on her side and fallen asleep.

He watched her for a moment, counting the heartbeats it took for her chest to rise and fall, and marveled at this new, protective urge he felt. Hawk had always been a caretaker, that much was true, but those he looked after tended to be his employees, or his customers. He couldn't remember the last time he felt this way toward a single person. He couldn't even remember the last time he had a non-business partner in anything but the most basic sense, yet here was Amalie.

A week ago he hadn't known her name. Now, he couldn't imagine what he would do if she was taken from him.

Hawk shook his head to clear it, then he left the infirmary. He debated locking the door, but he didn't know how long it would be until Amalie and Iveta woke, or how they would react to being trapped in such a small space. He also didn't know how his staff would react to the news of two vampires asleep in the back room. Then again, his staff had seen some crazy shit in the clubs he ran. And if Marek's forces tracked Amalie here, they would need to know the truth.

"There you are," Peter, the club's manager, said to Hawk as he jogged over to him. "I've been trying to call you all day."

"Sorry," Hawk began, but Peter waved it away.

"Don't worry about it. I've got all good news, boss—what they're calling a gas line explosion a few blocks over clearly wasn't," he continued. "I don't know what happened to the glass shop, but there's no danger to the club. We can remain open as usual."

"That's great," Hawk said. "We need to close down."

"Excuse me?" Peter said. "Has something happened?"

"What hasn't happened?" Hawk countered. "Amalie, the owner of the glass shop? Her ex-husband is the one who destroyed it. She and her assistant are in our infirmary, and I fear the madman might come after her."

"If the ex-husband is a threat, then we will keep him out," Peter said. His mind worked lightning fast, and he'd never met a problem he couldn't beat. It was why Hawk paid him a small fortune to keep his businesses running, and Peter was worth every koruna. "Any idea when this guy might be coming by?"

"After dark," Hawk replied. "Also, he's a vampire, as are Amalie and Iveta."

Peter blew out a breath. "Of course they are. Having to protect regular people would be boring, right?"

"If there's anything we don't do, it's boring," Hawk said. "Ideas?"

"I'll order a few sacks of garlic from the market, and send someone over to Saint Clement's for some holy water. Think we can use the bar's toothpicks for stakes?"

"I don't know if stakes work in real life the same way they do on film," Hawk replied, remembering how Amalie had walked toward him in the sunlight with no ill effects. Then he recalled her telling him that when she was a younger vampire, the sun had burned her quite badly, and she couldn't go out during the day for several years. She had also mentioned that Marek's forces we made up of mostly younger vampires. Hawk looked toward the ceiling at the array of stage lights, and asked, "Peter, how bright do these lights get?"

"They'll light up the place like high noon on a cloudless day," Peter replied. "We only turn them up all the way at the end of the night, to clear the place out. They're so powerful they make the main stage hot enough to fry eggs on the floor."

Hawk cocked an eyebrow. "Think they can get hot enough to fry a vampire?"

Peter grinned. "You bet, boss."

Chapter Eleven

Amalie - Prague, Present Day

AMALIE BLINKED HERSELF AWAKE, and felt a momentary surge of dread. The sterile room she was in and the hard cot beneath her reminded her of a hospital; if she'd ended up in a human emergency ward again, she would probably need to upend her life and leave Prague for the next hundred years. She liked her life here, and she liked what she and Iveta had rescued from the ashes of their former existence as Marek's playthings.

Just as Amalie was about to descend into panic, she saw a flyer taped to the wall about an upcoming event at the Moravian Ballroom. She remembered what had happened after the explosion, and smiled.

Hawk had brought her and Iveta to his club.

Despite the fact that her home was gone and her dearest friend lay unconscious beside her, Amalie was filled with happiness. It had been a long time since she'd known someone she could count on the way she trusted Hawk, and she liked the feeling. In fact, the last time an ally had presented themselves to her it had been Iveta herself, back in the early days when they first plotted to escape Marek. Amalie reached across the cot and grasped Iveta's hand, remembering the servant her cruel husband had assigned to her as a punishment. Little had Marek known that once Iveta was by her side, Amalie would be his downfall.

Chapter Twelve

Amalie - Marek's Camp, Before

"I don't need a handmaiden," Amalie hissed.

"I disagree, songstress. Since you cannot help but cause trouble wherever you go, I've assigned someone to watch over you," Marek said. Amalie had been caught giving the human cattle clean water and blankets again, and no act of kindness went unpunished in the warlord's camp. "She will be your shadow, and she will report to me on everything you do."

With that, Marek's men flung a filthy human girl into her room, and shut and locked the door behind them. Amalie helped the girl to her feet, and asked her what her name was.

"Iveta," she ground out. "And the bastard lied. I will do nothing to help him. Kill me if you want, but a vampire will never rule me."

"I am also a vampire," Amalie said, "but I hate Marek, as well. All he does is ruin things."

Iveta regarded Amalie, and asked, "Did he ruin you?"

"Yes," Amalie whispered. "In many, many ways."

Iveta lifted her chin, and Amalie saw resolve dancing in her eyes. "Will you help me escape?"

"Only if I can come with you." With that declaration, Amalie and Iveta were beholden to one another.

From that day onward, Amalie became the ideal woman in Marek's eyes. She ceased arguing with him, and whenever he summoned her she arrived quickly and without complaint. His advisors praised him for the iron control he exhibited over his woman, and they complimented both her singing voice and her lovely form. While Amalie distracted Marek and his guards, Iveta quietly befriended the castle's servants. Within a few months, they knew exactly who supported Marek, and who hated him almost as much as they did.

"How can you bear being near him for so long?" Iveta asked her one morning. Amalie had spent the entire night standing next to Marek's throne, either singing or otherwise acting as an ornament. "At least he didn't take you to bed."

"That's the only thing I enjoy about him." Marek was a terrible ruler, but an excellent lover. "If only he cared for his people the way he cares for those he sleeps with, he would be the sort of king bards sung about for centuries after he's gone."

"Why don't you rule?"

Amalie paused, and glanced at Iveta. "There is no way that would ever happen."

"Why not?" Iveta pressed. "All of Marek's people adore you, and they despise him! We've spent all of this time planning how to get away from him, but what if he's the one who needs to go?"

"I don't know," Amalie said, shaking her head. "Marek calls himself a warlord, but it's his mother, Varushka, that holds the true power. She's the clan's ruler, not him."

"Then she is the one we need to usurp."

The next night, Marek didn't hold court as he usually did. Instead, he sent his advisors away and took Amalie to bed.

"Why so attentive?" she asked, as they lounged together among the cushions. "What have I done to earn such affections?"

He kissed the soft spot behind her ear. "Am I too affectionate?"

"Never."

"You've really settled into this life," Marek continued. "You have become an asset to my court. In time, I might make you my true queen."

"My lord," Amalie said, bowing her head. "Truly, nothing would please me more."

"Nothing at all?" Marek asked, as his hands roamed across her body.

"Well, that always pleases me."

Marek laughed, a low rumble in his chest that affected Amalie more than she cared to admit. "Yes, you will be a good queen."

"But, what of your mother?" she asked; all the surrounding clans knew that Marek's mother, Lady Varushka, was the true leader of the family. "Would our lady approve of me, born a mere peasant, being granted such a noble title?"

"My mother will not question me. Don't mention her again while we're in bed. Makes my cock go soft."

Marek rolled Amalie underneath him, and she murmured, "As you wish, my lord."

"Husband," he said between thrusts. "Call me husband."

The next evening, Amalie smiled as she readied herself for court. If she became Marek's queen she could influence him, perhaps enough to change his ways. He'd even allayed her concerns about Varushka holding Amalie's low born status against her. If Amalie created a better life for both the vampire and human members of the clan, she and Iveta wouldn't need to escape. Amalie could live as she'd always dreamed, and, in time, she could return Iveta to her family. Everyone could finally live the sort of life they wanted.

There was also the fact that Amalie was enjoying this newer, more loving version of Marek. When she'd given herself to him all those years ago, it had been a desperate attempt to leave her village. Now she wondered if Marek's side was where she'd always belonged.

When Amalie entered the hall that evening, the usually boisterous crowd was tense, and focused on something happening near Marek's throne. Amalie made her way through the press of bodies, and gasped.

Iveta was chained to the whipping post.

"What's happening?" Amalie blurted out.

"Our lord has chosen another girl to change," one of the soldiers replied. "I like this one. Good tits."

Amalie glared at him, then she forced her way through the crown and found Marek. "Why are you doing this to Iveta?" she demanded.

"If you're to be my primary wife, and my queen, you will need a servant who's like us," he replied. "I'm changing her so you may keep her with you always."

"No, no, no," Amalie said. "Iveta doesn't want to be changed. Let her remain human, and I will find another servant."

"I've made my choice, Amalie," Marek said, then he stepped onto the platform. Before Amalie's eyes he grabbed the back of Iveta's dress and ripped it apart, leaving her naked body on display. As the crowd called out and jeered Marek bit her neck so violently blood gushed down her side, and soaked the ground beneath the platform. When Iveta was near death he slashed his wrist with his fangs and pressed it to her mouth, forcing her to drink.

Forcing her to become something she never wanted to be.

Varushka approached Amalie, and watched as Marek's blood dragged Iveta's spirit back to this side of the veil. "Next, he'll take her to his chamber and fuck her back to life, just like he did to you," Varushka said.

Amalie nodded as tears streamed down her cheeks. "I remember."

She patted Amalie's hand. "I know Iveta is special to you. That's why I ordered Marek to change her."

"Y-You did?" Amalie faced Varushka. "But why would you do such a thing?"

"Because I am the queen, and I can have whomever I want changed," Varushka snapped. "I know you have designs of becoming Marek's primary wife. His consort, if you will." Varushka touched the blood red garnet that rested in the hollow of her throat. "Make no mistake, little one, I rule the clan. No matter how pretty your voice is, or how many ways you let my son defile you, I will always be his queen. You are nothing."

Amalie gasped, but held her tongue. She knew better than to argue with Varushka in the hall where dozens of soldiers stood ready to defend her. They would cut off Amalie's head first, and ask questions later, if at all. No, she needed to be careful, and patient.

"As you say, my lady." Amalie bowed her head. Varushka smiled, and moved on through the crowd. As soon as she was gone Amalie turned back to the platform; the guards were cutting down Iveta's blood soaked body, then they carried her off the platform and away from view. Amalie knew she was being brought to Marek's special chamber, but not the one where he slept. The one where he destroyed.

Iveta was dumped onto the floor in the servant's wing shortly before sunrise. Those loyal to Amalie collected her, and brought the barely living girl to Amalie's chamber. They laid her on Amalie's bed, and brought hot water for a bath, and clear broth for Iveta to sip as soon as she was awake. Amalie and the rest of her handmaidens remembered the change well, and understood that once Iveta woke she would be ravenous, but too weak to consume blood for some time yet. That nightmare was yet to come. It was a nightmare Amalie had lived in for longer than she cared to think about.

And so Amalie cleaned and dressed Iveta's wounds, and the rest of the servants took on Iveta's duties and distracted the overseers so she had time to heal. Two full days after she'd been returned to Amalie, Iveta opened her eyes.

"I will destroy him for this," Iveta rasped, her ravaged throat still only partly healed.

"We will," Amalie promised. "Varushka, too."

Chapter Thirteen

Hawk - Prague,
Present Day

When Hawk returned to the infirmary, he found Amalie awake and sitting on the cot with her back against the wall. Iveta was sprawled out on the cot beside her, with her head lying in Amalie's lap.

"How is she?" Hawk asked.

Amalie cocked an eyebrow at him. "Asking after Iveta before me?"

"You are obviously feeling better." Hawk leaned over and kissed Amalie. "Tell me what you need."

"We're good," Amalie said, then Iveta rolled onto her back and cracked an eyelid.

"A coffee would be great," Iveta said. "Sugar, no milk. Some food would be nice, too. I assume you do feed your guests?"

"I have coffee already made upstairs," he said. "Can you walk?"

"Of course," Iveta said, then she stood and offered a hand to Amalie. "Food?"

"We have food in the kitchens, or we can have something delivered." Amalie looped her arm with Hawk's; he hadn't realized how much he needed to touch her, to know she was all right, until she did that. He kissed the top of her head, and asked, "Are you feeling better?"

"I am." She smiled up at him. "Thank you, for taking care of us."

"Thank him later," Iveta said. "I'm starving."

Hawk brought them to the glass walled office he and Amalie had shared the night before. The room had been thoroughly cleaned, and to Hawk's eyes it appeared to have never been used. Iveta took one step inside the room, breathed deeply, and narrowed her eyes at Amalie.

"Here, really?" she demanded. "He couldn't be bothered to bring you to a proper bedroom?"

"Iveta," Amalie said, her cheeks scarlet. "It wasn't like that!"

Iveta took another deep breath. "Oh, yes it was. And you," she said, rounding on Hawk. "You fuck where you keep your food?"

"Ahem." Hawk felt his own face warm. "This is a private room reserved for me and my special guests. It has a wet bar, and a fridge."

"And a very comfortable couch," Amalie added.

"I am not sitting on that, not after what you two did." Iveta went to the coffee machine and began pouring mugs. "What happened while we were out?"

"We've begun reinforcing the club." Hawk went to the corner cabinet and withdrew a floor plan of the Moravian Ballroom, and spread it out on the table. "Peter—he's my manager—has had all of the secondary entrances blocked. The only way in or out is through the front. That way, we can control how many of Marek's people get inside, and how quickly. Also, we've put the word out that we're closed tonight for a special event. Peter also obtained a few gallons of holy water. I'm not sure what he plans on doing with that; putting it in the sprinkler system, maybe?" He looked up, saw Amalie and Iveta's bewildered faces. "What?"

"Why are you leading Marek here?" Amalie asked.

"You said his followers are young and inexperienced," Hawk began. "Peter and I have put together a plan to lure them inside and, well, destroy them." When neither woman spoke, Hawk asked, "Isn't that what you want?"

"Yes, but why are *you* doing this?" Amalie pressed. "This isn't your problem."

"I disagree. I made you meet me here, in public. You were reticent, but I was desperate to know you, and because of my insistence I may have compromised your safety, and the safety of your people," Hawk replied. "I need to make this right."

Amalie stood on her toes and kissed his cheek. "Thank you, Hawk. You don't know what this means to me."

Hawk grasped her hand. "It's nothing."

Iveta rolled her eyes. "Both of you, stop. Where's this food you promised me?"

Chapter Fourteen

Amalie - Prague,
Present Day

Since Iveta refused to eat in the office, Hawk brought them down to the kitchens where Henri was in the midst of making the crew's lunch. As was his habit, he'd prepared more than enough food for all of them. The food was delicious, but Amalie thought the best part of her meal at Hawk's club was the wide-eyed shock across his, Peter, and Henri's faces.

"Have these three never eaten with women before?" Iveta asked, as she jerked her head toward the three mortals.

"I've never seen anyone eat so much," Hawk said. Amalie and Iveta had each eaten three roast beef sandwiches, a plate of dumplings and sauerkraut, and they were now sharing a blueberry kolache. By contrast, Hawk and Henri had only eaten one sandwich each, and Peter only had a cup of coffee and an apple.

"My mother eats like this," Henri said. "She used to roast three chickens for dinner. One for her, two for the rest of us. Not to mention the potatoes she put out with dinner, the vegetable casseroles, and at least an entire loaf of bread. Fresh baked," he added.

"We need a lot of nourishment when we're healing," Amalie explained. "Otherwise we can go for days or sometimes weeks without mortal food."

"How do you heal?" Peter asked. When Iveta growled, he held up his hands and said, "I didn't mean to pry!"

"You're not prying," Amalie said. "Iveta is just protective. Some would say overly protective," she added, with a knowing glance toward her friend.

"My protectiveness has kept your fool ass alive all this time," Iveta grumbled, as she speared the last dumpling with her knife and ate it directly from the blade.

"And what a fantastic ass it is," Hawk said.

Amalie smiled at Hawk, then she focused on Peter. "It's the blood that heals us."

"Will only vampire blood do the trick, or will any hemoglobin do?" he asked.

"Technically, all blood heals us. Blood is life, no?"

"There at the beginning and the end," Peter said, and Amalie nodded.

"While we could heal by drinking mortal blood, it would take a lot of blood, and be quite messy." Amalie grinned, and added, "The victims, they tend to squirm."

Peter laughed a bit too loudly. "You're kidding, right?"

"Am I?" Amalie countered. "Vampire blood is more concentrated than animal or even human blood. It is thicker, sweeter, and more powerful. The price of all that power—healing, our speed and strength, all of it—is exhaustion, followed by a ravenous appetite once we wake."

"Is that why some think vampires sleep all day?" Hawk asked. "Not because you fall into a stupor while the sun's out?"

"Yes, my brilliant one," Amalie replied. "In reality we're just tired."

"And when you wake you're ravenous for food?" Peter asked. "Not more blood, right?"

"I could go for some more blood," Iveta said. "But this kolache is delicious."

Henri leaned toward Iveta. "You're scaring him."

Iveta batted her eyelashes at the big, burly bouncer. "I know. Aren't you scared?"

"I don't scare easily."

"You will."

"If you're all done tormenting each other," Hawk began, casting a stern look at Henri but not Iveta, because he was no fool and wanted to stay alive for at least a few more decades, "it will be dark soon. Does anyone have more ideas on how we can lure these youngling vampires into the club?"

"Oh, I made some flyers," Peter said, then he withdrew one from his leather portfolio. It was an image of the interior of the club, with spotlights trained on an empty stage. Across the top of the flyer was the announcement "The Nightingale Sings: One Night Only".

"I'm going to sing?" Amalie asked.

"I believe your voice will be the perfect lure," Peter replied. "According to Hawk—well, according to nearly everyone in Old Town—your voice is legendary. We can route the sound from the microphone to the outdoor speakers, so anyone passing by will hear you. My theory is that your, um, enemy will recognize your voice, and send his soldiers in after you."

"When they're inside, I will lock the doors and bang!" Henri said. "Up go the lights."

"Lights?" Amalie asked, her gaze darting between the manager and bouncer. "What will a few lights do?"

"The stage lights are quite hot," Peter said. "If the soldiers are newly turned, as Hawk suggested they are, the lights should be hot enough to burn them, or at least disorient them long enough for us to come up with another plan."

"And then what?" Iveta asked.

Peter blinked. "What, what?"

"After you have a club full of burned and disoriented vampires, then what?" Iveta pressed. "Are you going to dump oil on them, fry them up like chicken cutlets? Or just leave them in here, screaming and stinking and planning how to murder you?"

"W-We thought they would burn down to ashes," Peter said. Iveta began to argue, but Amalie held up her hand.

"They won't die," Amalie told them. "At least, not that way. I understand what you're trying to do, and I appreciate it. Truly, I do; it's been so long since anyone other than Iveta wanted to help me, I'd almost forgotten how good it feels. Thank you, each of you." Hawk reached across the table and squeezed her hand.

"While the lights won't kill them, the younglings will be gravely injured," she continued. "It will give Iveta enough time to alert the rest of my people, and get them to safety."

"I am not leaving you!" Iveta made a cutting motion with her hand. "No!"

"You are the only one who can get to them in time," Amalie said. "Even I'm not as fast as you. You're their only hope."

Iveta looked away. "And, then what? We will relocate somewhere new while you sacrifice yourself to Marek?"

"No," Hawk said, his voice booming in the near-empty club. "If the heat from the lights won't kill Marek's soldiers, what will?"

"Not much," Amalie said. "Even the newly made are strong. Fire will kill them, decapitation—"

"Sounds messy," Peter said.

Amalie nodded. "Yes. Quite messy."

"Starvation," Iveta said. "If they're already weak from the hot lights, lock them in. Without any nourishment, they'll turn on each other."

"How long will it take them to die?" Hawk asked.

"Depends on how many there are," Iveta said with a shrug. "Five will decimate each other in a day, maybe two. More will last longer."

"How long would, say, two dozen last?" Hawk pressed.

"A week, perhaps."

"How long would you last, locked in with two dozen starving vampires?" Henri asked. "Would you survive for an entire week?"

Iveta looked him dead in the eye. "I would kill them all, and use their bones to dig my way to freedom."

"She's done it before," Amalie said. "Henri, you and Peter should go with Iveta. You'll be safer with her and the rest of my people. You too, Hawk."

They both looked to Hawk. "Amalie is right," Hawk said. "You two should go."

"And you," Amalie said, but he shook his head.

"You need me here," he said. "Do you know how to work the sound equipment? Or where the controls are for the lights? No, you don't."

Amalie pursed her lips at Hawk, her infuriating, stubborn, wonderful man. "If you die it's your own fault. I won't mourn you, not for a single second."

"Then I had better not die." Hawk stood, and began stacking up empty plates. "Since we want the vampires to starve, we should probably empty out the fridge and the concession stand before nightfall."

After Iveta left to meet the clan, with her two mortal men in tow, Amalie stood in the club's DJ booth and gazed at the empty dance floor. The Moravian Ballroom was massive, easily twice as large as its namesake dance halls, and despite Hawk's confidence she agreed with Iveta. There was only a very small chance that this plan would go well. There was a much larger chance that either Amalie or Hawk would die.

And, of course, there was a strong chance they would die together.

A chill rolled down her spine. Amalie rubbed warmth back into her arms as Hawk entered the booth, his boots making hollow sounds against the metal floor. He embraced her from behind, and she leaned back into the comfort of him.

"We're both going to die," Amalie declared.

He kissed the soft spot behind her ear. "Will you dance with me in the afterlife?"

"No. I will yell at you for being so foolish as to get involved with vampires."

"Then we'll dance after the yelling?"

Amalie tried not to smile, but Hawk's confidence made it difficult. Add to that the soft kisses he pressed to her neck, and it was almost impossible. "Do you take anything seriously?"

"On the contrary," Hawk said, his warm breath sending shivers down her skin, "I am very serious about kissing you." Amalie laughed, and turned to face him.

A crash sounded overhead. Hawk shoved Amalie behind him as Marek burst through the skylight amid a shower of broken glass. With a single hand Marek sent Hawk hurtling out of the booth and skidding across the dance floor. Amalie lunged after Hawk, but Marek grabbed her shoulder.

"I was told you would be singing, my nightingale," Marek growled, his fingers digging into her flesh as he used his other hand to drag his sharp, talon-like fingernails down her neck. "It's been so long since I've heard your lovely voice."

"Not long enough." Amalie spat at his feet, but made no move to evade him. She hoped if Marek kept his attention on her, Hawk would have time to escape. As always, Marek knew her next move almost before she did.

"Thinking to shield your mortal?" Marek struck as fast as a viper, and had her by the neck as her feet dangled above the floor. "Don't worry. I'll kill him, but not until after I kill you."

Amalie raised her hands, but Marek grabbed both of wrists one handed, while the other began ripping her sweater apart. "I've missed your fire, Nightingale. Now give me my garnet."

Chapter Fifteen

Hawk - Prague,
Present Day

Hawk groaned as he came back to himself, with every muscle and bone in his body screaming in protest. As his wits returned, he remembered: a man falling through the ceiling, wickedly sharp pieces of glass, him hitting the floor and sliding away from—

Amalie.

Slowly, he moved his head so he could see the DJ booth. The man—Marek, he assumed—didn't notice Hawk. Marek's attention was on Amalie, whom he held by the throat as he raked his claws down her back and side. His brave nightingale didn't make a sound, but the thought didn't fill Hawk with pride. Amalie was amazingly strong, and this Marek had easily overpowered her. That meant that Hawk wouldn't stand a chance against the vampire physically. Luckily, Hawk's greatest strength had always been his mind.

He glanced around the club, searching for a suitable weapon, when he spied the foam machine they used for college raves. Hawk had been against the idea of foam parties from the beginning and flat out refused to purchase one of the expensive commercial machines, so Peter had cobbled one together with a leaf blower and a pressure washer. It hadn't worked very well, which was why they'd only hosted the one foam party. Hawk remembered the massive puddles of water the machine had left behind...

...and that the DJ booth had a metal floor.

Hawk raised himself into a crouch, and crept to the side of the dance floor. Hoping Marek hadn't noticed him, he swung himself onto the metal scaffolding and climbed up to the catwalks. Mounted along the railings were dozens of lights. Several of them were mounted right above Marek's head. But before Hawk could deal with the lights, he needed to turn on the foam.

There was a secondary control panel on the center catwalk. Walking as quietly as possible, Hawk activated the foam machine, and used the joystick to angle the spray toward the booth. Marek glanced at the water accumulating around his boots, then ignored it so he could continue torturing Amalie.

"Bastard," Hawk muttered as he turned up the spray. That done, he continued on down the catwalk until he reached the main spotlight directly above the DJ booth. Hoping he wouldn't accidentally kill himself, Hawk pulled the cable out of the back of the light's can, and yelled, "Metal floor!"

Marek looked up, annoyed and snarling and just distracted enough for Amalie to twist out of his grasp.

Hawk dropped the cable.

Amalie caught it, and shoved it onto Marek's neck beneath his bearskin cape.

Hawk hit the power as Amalie jumped out of the booth and onto the dance floor.

Marek screamed as his body shook, then he was silent.

Hawk cut the power to the spotlight, then he scrambled down the scaffolding and onto the dance floor. He found Amalie lying on her side in a pool of foam. Blood from the long gashes in her skin had tinted the foam pink, and her clothes were shredded down to rags. Gingerly, Hawk gathered her in his arms.

"Careful," he said when she tried to push herself up. "Give yourself a minute. He's dead."

"Doubtful," Amalie whispered. "But it's a nice thought."

"He was ripping you apart," Hawk said.

"Not me, my clothes. Marek wanted the garnet, but he didn't find it." Hawk glanced at her breast, since the last he knew the garnet was hidden in her bra. Amalie smiled, and said, "It's not here. I made Iveta take it with her."

"My brilliant one." Hawk pushed the damp hair back from her forehead. "Does this mean Iveta's now in charge of the entire clan?"

"When wasn't she?" Amalie countered. "Come on. We need to assess the state of the warlord." Hawk helped Amalie up, groaning as he felt his own injuries. She cast a sharp glance toward him, but he waved it away. "Is the power off?" she asked, her foot hovering above the metal floor.

"Yes." Leaning on each other, they looked into the DJ booth. Marek lay sprawled across the floor, the skin on his face and neck bloody and charred. "You really think he'll survive this?"

"As a species we're very hard to kill. However, he won't be going anywhere for a while."

"What of his followers?"

"If they're not here now, they're not coming until after dark. How long until sunset?"

Hawk checked his watch. "Four hours."

"Then we have time." Amalie led Hawk back to the infirmary located in the rear of the club. Once they were inside the room she ordered him to sit on the cot, and take off his shirt.

"Checking me for wounds?" he asked, as she stroked her hands across his arms and back.

"Marek threw you very far," she replied. "You might have fractures."

"When he threw me, his hand wasn't on me," Hawk said. "He never touched me."

"No, he didn't." When Hawk's brows pinched, she winked at him. "Patience. I can't tell you all of our secrets, not right away. Don't you want a woman with some mystery?" she added, then she pulled off the remains of her sweater and straddled his waist.

"Now?" Despite his words, he settled his hands on her hips. "But you're hurt."

"As are you." Amalie slashed her nails across the thin skin under her throat. When the blood welled to the surface, she said, "Drink."

"No," he protested, leaning away. "You need your strength."

"I need your strength, too." When he remained still, mesmerized by thick red droplets, she said, "I'm not trying to turn you. I'd never do that, not unless you wanted it, and even then I'd try to convince you to remain mortal."

"It's not that," he said, gutted that she thought he'd been wary of her. "I was thinking the blood looks like a ruby necklace." He cocked his head to the side. "Is that why your leaders wear a blood red garnet?"

She smiled, and all but shoved his face into her breast. "Look at you, divining all my secrets on your own. Now drink, so you'll live to figure out a few more."

Chapter Sixteen

After they'd taken the time to rest and clean up as well as they could, talk turned to what should be done about Marek.

"As much as it would make my life easier, we shouldn't kill him," Amalie said. They'd raided Hawk's office for clothes, and she was wearing one of his dress shirts over the remains of her jeans. The sleeves were rolled up past the elbows, and the hem of the shirt almost reached her knees. "I need him alive so I can send a message to his camp."

"A corpse sends a rather specific message." Hawk stood over Marek's nearly dead form with his arms crossed over his chest and his stance wide. Amalie didn't say as much, but in that pose Hawk reminded her of the vampire hunters from the old days. "He tried to kill you. Right in front of me, he tried to rip you apart. Why should he get to live?"

"Because his failure, coupled with his survival, will be humiliating, and for Marek humiliation is a fate worse than death." Amalie placed her hands on Hawk's chest. "It will also prove, beyond any doubt, that I remain more powerful than Marek. Only Varushka could have hurt Marek as badly as this, and she's long since dead."

Hawk grunted. "I suppose, since you've made a name for yourself by ripping out throats and defeating warlords, I shouldn't argue with you."

Amalie stood on her toes, and slid her hands onto Hawk's shoulders. "Hawk, you have nothing to fear from me. Not ever."

He rested his forehead against hers. "I know, my beauty. Let's get this bastard out of my club."

Of course, they needed to find a way to move Marek while simultaneously concealing his burned body. After much trial and error, they rolled him up in an old rug and carried him out on their shoulders.

"Such a cliché," Amalie lamented, as they hauled their gruesome cargo down the narrow streets and toward the Vltava, the wide river that ran through Prague.

"We could have chopped him up and stuffed him in garbage bags," Hawk said. Even though he brought up the rear of the rug, Amalie held up the bulk of Marek's weight. "Would he regenerate from that?"

"Perhaps, in time," Amalie said. "And only if the pieces weren't too small."

"Next time, we chop," Hawk grunted. "I'll have my butcher knife ready."

"I am sure you will." They stepped onto the shore, and Amalie's boots made a sucking sound against the mud. "Careful. It's slippery."

"It would be tragic if I dropped Marek and he broke his neck."

"Hawk!"

They left Marek at the very edge of the river, still loosely rolled up in the carpet. Amalie looked across the wide expanse of water, and sighed. "When I was young, we called this the wild waters."

"How long ago was that?"

"Long enough." She nudged the carpet onto the rockier part of the foreshore with her boot. While she wanted Marek to survive this latest ordeal, she did not want him to be comfortable. "Let's go to the bridge, and watch."

As the river lapped at Marek tight in his rug, Amalie led Hawk to the Charles Bridge. As ever, it was packed with tourists. They chose a spot alongside one of the grand old statues that lined either side of the bridge, and watched the carpet as it lay on the foreshore. From that distance it looked like nothing more than a cast off bit of rubbish, not the body of the once-fierce vampire warlord that held all of Eastern Europe in check.

"Will his people find him before the tide comes in?" Hawk asked.

Amalie shrugged. "They will, or they won't. If he drowns, so be it. I won't miss him."

"Did you ever love him?"

"No," she replied without hesitation. "I loved the idea of leaving my boring village behind, and I loved the idea of being a powerful queen. But while Marek did take me from my home, I was never more than a plaything to him. I was a shiny bauble in a court already packed with shiny baubles. While I was with him, I was nothing."

Hawk brought her hand to his mouth and kissed her knuckles. "Amalie, you were never nothing."

She smiled at him, this mortal man she'd wanted nothing to do with and had avoided at all costs. And yet, Hawk had pushed his way into her life, and even though they'd only shared a handful of days together Amalie couldn't imagine her life without him. She wondered how long he would be willing to put up with a vampire.

Maybe not forever, but for a good while?

Amalie moved closer to him, intending to tell Hawk how she felt but not having the slightest idea how to begin, when he jerked his chin toward the riverbank.

"They found him."

With one graceful movement Amalie got on top of the stone wall, her black hair streaming in the wind behind her. She observed as Marek's soldiers first unrolled him from the sodden, filthy carpet, and then as they began opening their wrists and dripping blood into his mouth to try and revive him.

"Do they know you're here?" Hawk asked.

"They know."

She'd no sooner said the words when one of the soldiers looked up, and saw Amalie standing on the bridge's side wall. He alerted the rest of the soldiers, and they momentarily stopped tending to Marek as they stared incredulously at the small, lowborn woman who had bested the legendary warlord two times now. Three times, if you counted Varushka's death.

Amalie counted it. She still remembered the warm spray of Varushka's blood on her face, and the weak, stuttering heartbeats as her life slipped away. Amalie would never forget the slow, messy death of her worst enemy.

Now Amalie stood tall on the Charles Bridge, and lifted her chin as Marek's soldiers stood on the banks of the Vltava. There were five soldiers clustered around Marek, and if they attacked now neither she nor Hawk would stand a chance. But the soldiers didn't know that. All they knew was that Marek lay at their feet, very, very close to death, while an apparently uninjured Amalie watched them from above.

Hesitantly, the soldier that first noticed her bowed. The other four followed suit, their stiff movements telling Amalie that they didn't know if they would survive the night if they were seen rescuing Marek. She nodded to the five, and watched as they straightened, then gathered up Marek and carried him away. None of the soldiers dared meet her gaze again.

"That was stressful," Hawk grumbled, shattering the tense mood. "Are all you vampires so dramatic?"

Amalie laughed, and let him help her down from the wall and into his arms. "We are. Think you can handle it?"

"For you, I can handle anything."

<<<The End>>>

More Books in the Bound by Blood Series
The Sacrifice and the Spare, an MF arranged marriage romance by Elle Backenstoe
The Tainted and the Tamed, an MF slow-burn, class difference romance by C.K. Beggan
The Stars and the Stage, an NB/M second chance enemies-to-lovers romance by D. N. Bryn
The Hawk and the Nightingale, an MF forbidden love romance by Jennifer Allis Provost
The Magnolia and the Bleeding Heart, an FFF second chance mafia romance by River Bennet
The Nettle and the Nightmare, an FFM enemies-to-lovers romance by Alora Black
The Thorn and the Thistle, an MF forbidden romance by Kendra Corbeau
The Moon and the Hunt, an MF fated mates second chance romance by Ophelia Wells Langley

ALSO BY JENNIFER ALLIS PROVOST

The Chronicles of Parthalan, a six volume epic fantasy (and one short story collection)
Heir to the Sun
The Virgin Queen
Rise of the Deva'shi
Pieces of Parthalan: Six All-New Stories From The Land Of
Parthalan
Golem
Elfsong
Sunfall

The Copper Legacy, a four book urban fantasy:
Copper Girl
Copper Ravens
Copper Veins
Copper Princess
A duology based in the Copper world:
Redemption
Salvation
Poison Garden, an urban fantasy filled with seers, witches, and one seriously hot detective:
Belladonna
Oleander
Bleeding Hearts
Thornapple

Wolfsbane

Gallowglass, an urban fantasy set in Scotland and New York:

Gallowglass

Walker

Homecoming

Winter's Queen, an urban fantasy set in Scotland and Elphame:

Touch of Frost

Giant's Daughter

Elphame's Queen

Merrowkin, an urban fantasy set in Ireland above and below

Merrowkin

Death's Door

Manannán's Pearl

Changes, a contemporary romance:

Changing Teams

Changing Scenes

Changing Fate

Changing Dates

About the Author

Jennifer Allis Provost is a native New Englander who lives in a sprawling colonial along with her beautiful and precocious twins, a dog that thinks she's a kangaroo, a parrot, a junkyard cat, and a wonderful husband who never forgets to buy ice cream. As a child, she read anything and everything she could get her hands on, including a set of encyclopedias, but fantasy was always her favorite. She spends her days drinking vast amounts of coffee, arguing with her computer, and avoiding any and all domestic behavior.

Find Jenn on the web here: http://authorjenniferallisprovost.com/

For up to the minute sale notifications, follow her on Bookbub here: https://www.bookbub.com/profile/jennifer-allis-provost
For exclusive content, follow her on Patreon: https://www.patreon.com/jenniferallisprovost/
Friend her on Facebook: http://www.facebook.com/jennallis
Follow her on Instagram: @jenniferaprovost
Happy reading!